Where Are Momma, Poppa, and Sister June?

Story and Pictures by Dick Gackenbach

Clarion Books/*New York*

Clarion Books
a Houghton Mifflin Company imprint
215 Park Avenue South, New York, NY 10003
Text and illustrations copyright © 1994 by Dick Gackenbach

The illustrations for this book were executed in sepia pen and ink and watercolor
on D'arches paper.
The text was set in 20/25 pt. Bookman.

Library of Congress Cataloging-in-Publication Data

Gackenbach, Dick.
Where are Momma, Poppa, and Sister June? / by Dick Gackenbach.
p. cm.
ummary: A child worries about where the rest of the family went until a note is discov-
ered that explains everything.
ISBN 0-395-67323-2
[1. Family life—Fiction. 2. Worry—Fiction.] I. Title.
PZ7.G117Whe 1994

[E]—dc20   93-40809
                                                                                                      CIP

WOZ 10 9 8 7 6 5 4 3 2 1

for Tony Kramer

I knew something was wrong
when I got home from playing
baseball.
The house was empty.
It was very quiet.
No Momma,
no Poppa,
no sister June.

Momma should have been
cooking dinner.

Poppa should have been
watching the news.

Sister June should have been talking on the telephone.

What could have happened to them? I wondered.

Did a giant crocodile
eat them?

It has been known to happen.

11

Or maybe aliens came
and zapped them up into space.

That has been known to happen, too.

Or did the dreaded Swamp Critter
drag them away?

15

I bet I did something bad,
and they went off
and left me forever.

LoNG!

"Momma," I called.
"Poppa," I shouted.
"Sister June. Where are you?"
No one answered.
I was all alone!

19

I went to cry on Queenie's shoulder.
"Oh, Queenie," I said,
"what are we going to do?
They have gone away and left us."

Then I saw Queenie was chewing on something.
She was chewing up a note.
"Give that to me, Queenie," I cried.
"It's a kidnapper's note!"

23

I began to put the note together
piece by piece.
My heart was pounding.

25

I found a WE.
I found a HAVE GONE.
Then I found a FOR,
and an A.
And then, I found
a BE, and a BACK SOO.
What could it mean?
I wondered.

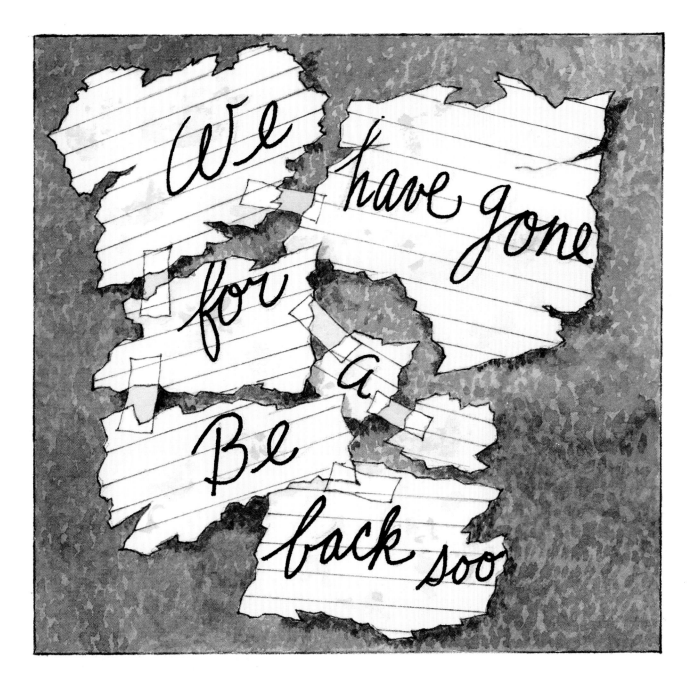

Suddenly the front door opened.
"We have the pizza," said Momma.
"Any calls for me?" asked my
sister June.
"I hope you found our note,"
said Poppa.

"Yes, I found it," I told him.
I didn't tell them how worried I was.

"And don't give Queenie any pizza,"
I said.

"AGH-H-H-H!"